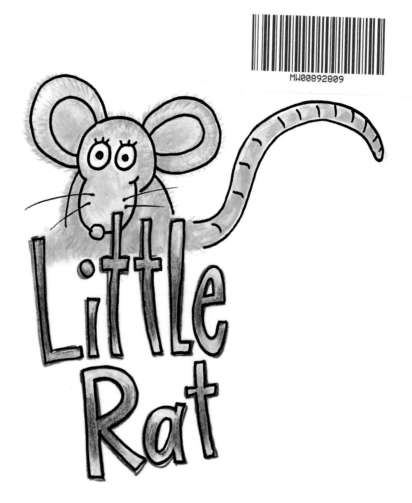

Little Rat

Written & Illustrated
by
Brad & Sarah Schaupeter

Colorizing & Graphics by
Cheryl Fontana

ISBN-10: 153091995
ISBN-13: 978-1530919970

To our daughter, Ruby

Little rat, little rat,
why are you like that?

Why do you lick my nose?
and then sometimes my toes?

Do you think it tastes good?
Or do you think it's just food?

I asked the little rat
why she likes this?
And she said,

"I don't know,
I guess because I like to kiss."

Little rat, little rat,
why are you
like that?

Why do you like to go through the trash?
Is it because I don't feed you enough?

Or do you like to dig through stuff?

I asked the little rat, why do you
go in the trash for apple cores? And she said,
"I don't know, I guess I just like to explore."

Little rat, little rat
why are you like that?
Why do you climb up high?

I asked the little rat, why do you like to climb so high? And she said. "I guess I just like to look you in the eye."

Little rat, little rat, why do you chew on things?

You chew the carpet,
and socks, and wires,
and homework,
and rings.

I asked the little rat, why do you chew so much?
She said,
"I don't know, I guess I simply like to munch."

Little rat, little rat, why are you like that?
Why do you steal my stuff and hide it
under the bed?
You steal my books,
and
my chap stick,

and my toilet paper,
and my pencil lead.

I asked little rat, why do you hide
these things under
the place where I rest?

She said, "Because I want your bed
to be just above my nest."

Little rat,
little rat,
why do you
follow me
wherever I go?

Do you think you're in
          a high speed chase?

Or maybe you think we're in
      a very fast foot race.

Little rat, little rat
why do you climb
all over me?

Do you think I'm a gymnasium
or a playscape?

Or maybe you think you're
a monkey or an ape?

I asked
the little rat,
why do you do
the things
you do?

And little rat said
"I guess I just
like to be
close to you."

Based on the true adventures
of our little rat

Made in the USA
San Bernardino, CA
27 March 2017